WOLVERINE 2007

Welcome to the Wolverine Annual 2007, Bub! I've left my mark on this annual and scratched 10 claw marks, just like this, within these pages! Use your powers of observation to see if you can find them all! I'll see you on page 62 and we can check if you're correct.

Good Luck!

CLAW MARKS

£6.99

CW00524758

THE HOTEL RIPLEY, NEW YORK, NEW YORK.

INVASION of the BODY SNATCHERS at the GEM THEATRE

GOOD AFTERNOON, SIR. WILL, YOU BE CHECKING IN WITH US TODAY?

NO...

CONTINUED ON PAGE 14

9

WOLVERINE

NAME: James Howlett, currently known as Logan
PUBLIC IDENTITY: Wolverine
HEIGHT: 5 feet 3 inches
AGE: Unknown

OVERALL RATING **9**

WOLVERINE		
STRENGTH:	4	
AGILITY:	6	
ENDURANCE:	8	
INTELLIGENCE:	3	
COMBAT SKILL:	9	
POWER:	3	
THREAT LEVEL:	9	

In order to create the perfect soldier, the Weapon X scientists bonded the indestructible metal adamantium to Wolverine

BACKGROUND>>>

Little is known of Logan's origin and due to his power of regeneration it is nearly impossible to determine his true age. What is known is that he was born James Howlett, son of a wealthy landowner in Alberta, Canada, in the later days of the 19th Century. James first discovered his mutant abilities when, as a young man, he witnessed

the murder of his father. His rage caused his claws to shoot out, stabbing his father's killer.
Overwhelmed by the horror of what had happened James fled into the wilds of Canada.
He then resurfaced many years later when he fought during World War II. After the war he became a CIA 'Black Ops' agent and, having spent many years in Japan, even trained as a Samurai – Japan's legendary warrior elite.

BACKGROUND CONTINUED>>>

Logan then volunteered for the Weapon X programme, a top secret US government operation designed to create super soldiers.
During an extremely painful operation, the scientists of Weapon X laced Logan's skeleton with the indestructible metal, adamantium.
In order to control Logan they erased his memories, however, his animal nature was too strong and he escaped. James and Heather Hudson of the Canadian super team Alpha Flight, found him and nursed him back to sanity. He later joined Canada's Department H where he was code-named Wolverine.
It was whilst at Department H that Wolverine was approached by Professor X, who recruited him for the X-Men.

After Magneto ripped all the adamantium from Wolverine's body, Wolverine's healing factor reached phenomenal levels and he grew bone claws.

Wolverine's rage gets the better of him as he attacks everyone's favourite friendly neighbourhood Spider-Man! He's even fought the Incredible Hulk!

Logan is a superb fighter and trained in many forms of martial arts. In combat however, he has a tendency of entering into a animalistic rage where he becomes a danger to not just his foes, but friends as well.

MUTANT POWERS >>>
ADAMANTIUM SKELETON, CLAWS, HEALING FACTOR, ENHANCED SENSES.

ADAMANTIUM SKELETON AND CLAWS >>>

Wolverine's skeleton is laced with adamantium, the strongest metal known to man and virtually indestructible, making his bones unbreakable. In addition, he is equipped with three retractable claws on each hand, which can cut through almost anything.

HEALING FACTOR >>>

Wolverine also possesses a healing factor. This ability allows him to regenerate from incredible injuries that would kill a normal man, including bullet wounds and being set on fire. His healing factor also makes him nearly immune to all poisons and diseases.

CLAW MARKS

ENHANCED SENSES >>>

Wolverine's sense of smell and hearing are superhumanly acute allowing him to track people just by their scent or detect a hidden assassin by their heartbeat.

MARVEL
FACTS

When the character for Wolverine was first proposed one of the name's suggested was The Badger!

Before Wolverine was unmasked this is what a teen Logan might have looked like.

Wolverine made his first appearance in Incredible Hulk #181, November 1974.

THE BROOD

Long tail with two poisonous stingers

Strong armour-like exoskeleton

Translucent wings

REAL NAME: Not Applicable
PUBLIC IDENTITY: Secret, the public are unaware of the Brood's existence.
HEIGHT: Approxiamately 8 feet

BACKGROUND:
The Brood are an evil, insect-like alien race with a hive mentality, very much like bees. Each Brood hiveship is ruled over by a Queen.

The Brood create more Brood by implanting eggs into host bodies. When these eggs hatch they turn the host body into a new Brood warrior. Only the strongest host bodies, however, are worthy of the egg of a Brood Queen.

The Brood have fought the X-Men on many occasions and have even managed to impregnate Wolverine with one of their eggs. Fortunately, Wolverine's healing factor saved him.

viscously sharp teeth

OVERALL RATING 7

BROOD WARRIOR		
STRENGTH:		4
AGILITY:		4
ENDURANCE:		5
INTELLIGENCE:		4
COMBAT SKILL:		7
POWER:		3
THREAT LEVEL:		7

SILVER SAMURAI

Able to generate a powerful tachyon field allowing his sword to cut through almost anything!

Expert sword master

NAME: KENIUCHIO HARADA
KNOWN ALIASES: ISHIRO TAGARA
HEIGHT: 6 feet 6 inches

Powerful armour

BACKGROUND:
The mutant son of the Japanese crimelord Shingen Harada, head of Clan Yashida, Keniuchio Harada mastered the disciplines of bushido (the Samurai code of chivalry) and became a mercenary. He first worked for the criminal Mandrill and fought Daredevil. Silver Samurai then served Viper, an agent of the terrorist organisation Hydra, as her bodyguard. In this capacity, he battled opponents such as Spider-Man amongst others.

Following his father's death, Silver Samurai sought to wrest control of Clan Yashida from his half-sister Mariko Yashida, but he was opposed by Mariko's lover, Wolverine.

After Mariko's death, Silver Samurai claimed clan leadership and briefly led the Japanese government's fledgling super-team, Big Hero 6. However, control of Clan Yashida was wrested from him by the Mongolian Kaishek crime family, and he allied himself with Wolverine to defeat them. The disgrace of losing leadership was too great for Silver Samurai, and he has since returned to a mercenary life.

OVERALL RATING 6

SILVER SAMURAI		
STRENGTH:		6
AGILITY:		4
ENDURANCE:		6
INTELLIGENCE:		4
COMBAT SKILL:		7
POWER:		3
THREAT LEVEL:		8

VILLAINS...

SABRETOOTH

REAL NAME: VICTOR CREED
KNOWN ALIASES: SABRETOOTH,
Also known as Der Schlater
(The Butcher), Slasher, El Tigre
HEIGHT: 6 feet 6 inches

Enhanced senses

Deadly claws

Healing factor

BACKGROUND:
Little is known of Victor Creed's early years, however, it is understood that around the 1910s, as an adult, Creed, now calling himself Sabretooth, fought with the young Logan and defeated him.

Many years later, during the 1960s, Sabretooth resurfaced as part of Team X, a covert operations unit run by the Central Intelligence Agency (C.I.A.) for the shadowy Weapon X program. Due to the C.I.A. wiping their memories, neither men remembered their previous encounter although their animosity towards each other caused numerous problems.

After Team X was disbanded Sabretooth became an international assassin. He also worked for the shape changer Mystique's Brotherhood of Mutants and was re-enlisted by the Weapon X program, who bonded the unbreakable alloy adamantium to his skeleton.

Over the years, Sabretooth and Wolverine have had a long-standing feud, and Sabretooth has taken every opportunity to torment his rival.

OVERALL RATING 8

SABRETOOTH	
STRENGTH:	6
AGILITY:	4
ENDURANCE:	6
INTELLIGENCE:	4
COMBAT SKILL:	7
POWER:	3
THREAT LEVEL:	8

BLOODSCREAM

NAME: UNREVEALED
KNOWN ALIASES: BLOODSPORT
HEIGHT: 6 feet 5 inches

Enhanced strength and healing

Vampiric touch

Zombie control

BACKGROUND:
Born in the mid-16th century, the man destined to become Bloodscream was a naval surgeon in Sir Francis Drake' armada. Mortally wounded in battle, he accepted the sorcerer Dagoo's offer to save his life but was instead transformed into a vampire-like creature. Learning that an elixir from the blood of a man who did not age was the only cure for his condition, Bloodscream became a soldier, hoping to encounter fellow immortals on the battlefield.

After centuries of combat, Bloodscream fought in the Battle of Normandy in 1944 where he encountered a Canadian soldier named Logan. Decades later, while working as an enforcer for the crimelord General Coy, Bloodscream clashed once more with Logan, now known as Wolverine. Realising that his foe had not aged since their last encounter, Bloodscream believed Wolverine's blood would serve in his elixir and free him from his curse. To this end Bloodscream has fought Wolverine on numerous occasions, even apparently being slain, but he has always survived due to his vampiric powers.

OVERALL RATING 7

BLOODSCREAM	
STRENGTH:	6
AGILITY:	4
ENDURANCE:	9
INTELLIGENCE:	4
COMBAT SKILL:	8
POWER:	3
THREAT LEVEL:	6

13

"HMPH, FIRST TIME I'VE EVER HEARD MYSELF TAGGED WITH *THAT* ONE. YA GOT A BEEF WITH THE BROOD I TAKE IT?"

ALTHOUGH JUST BEING ALIVE MEANS YA BASICALLY GOT A BEEF WITH THE BROOD.

SLEAZOIDS ARE THE SCOURGE OF THE GALAXY, HIJACKIN' INNOCENT FOLK TO TURN 'EM INTO HOST BODIES FOR THEIR *EGGS*.

ME AN' THE X-MEN HAVE HAD MORE THAN OUR FAIR SHARE OF SCRAPES WITH THEM BUGGERS, ONCE EVEN HAVING BEEN IMPLANTED WITH *BROOD QUEENS*.

IN FACT, EACH TIME WE FACED 'EM WE'VE BEEN *LUCKY* TO ESCAPE WITH OUR LIVES.

THE BROOD ARE ABOUT AS DEADLY AS THEY COME.

"IF BY THE TERM '*BEEF*' YOU MEAN I HAVE REASON TO *HATE* THEM, YOU ARE CORRECT."

I AM *TYRUS KRILL*. I AM WHAT TERRANS MIGHT CALL A *BOUNTY HUNTER*. TO BE MORE SPECIFIC, A BROOD BOUNTY HUNTER.

THEN I GATHER YOU AIN'T COME TO EARTH TO TAKE IN THE SIGHTS.

WERE IT ONLY SO.

A CERTAIN GROUP I HAVE BEEN TRACKING FOR YEARS HAVE MADE THEIR WAY HERE. THEY HAVE USED THE RECENT ACTIONS OF OTHER GALACTIC CULTURES AS AN OPPORTUNITY TO ESTABLISH A FOOT-HOLD HERE ON EARTH.

NEEDLESS TO SAY, YOUR WORLD'S POPULATION IS IN GRAVE DANGER.

WHAT *ELSE* IS NEW.

BUT IF YA DON'T MIND ME ASKIN', WHAT MAKES THESE PARTICULAR BROOD SO SPECIAL THAT YOU'VE BEEN FOLLOWIN' THEM FOR YEARS?

THEY ARE A RUTHLESS GROUP, EVEN FOR THE BROOD. THE BLOOD SPILLED OF THOSE THEY SLAY ARE NOT NECESSARILY FOR *REPRODUCTION*, BUT FOR *PLEASURE*.

EVEN AMONGST THE BROOD RACE ITSELF, THEY ARE CONSIDERED... *CRIMINALS*. BUT ON A MORE PERSONAL LEVEL...

...THEY ARE RESPONSIBLE FOR THE DEATH OF MY *FAMILY*.

I'M SORRY FOR YOUR LOSS, PAL...

...BUT I'M GUESSIN' YA DIDN'T GO THROUGH ALL THIS TROUBLE TO FIND ME TO HAVE ME CRY IN YOUR BEER WITH YA. YA CAME TO ME FOR *HELP*, AN' AS FAR AS THE BROOD'S CONCERNED, IT DON'T TAKE MUCH TO *GET* IT.

WHERE ARE THESE SLEAZOIDS AT?

THEY'VE MANAGED TO ENTRENCH THEMSELVES IN AN ESTABLISHMENT NAMED THE *RIPLEY HOTEL*, INSINUATING THEMSELVES AMONG THE HUMANS THERE.

OF COURSE, THAT COULD BE BUT THE *START*.

ONE OF THOSE I'VE BEEN FOLLOWING IS A *QUEEN*.

DON'T WORRY ABOUT IT, BUB--

15

IT FEELS AS IF I'VE BEEN HUNTING THESE MONSTERS FOREVER AND YET, THAT DAY REMAINS AS VISIBLE IN MY MIND AS IF IT OCCURRED YESTERDAY. THAT HORRIBLE DAY...

...WHEN MY WORLD CAME TO AN END.

SFFT

FATHER!

ZET, HOW MANY TIMES MUST I TELL YOU NOT TO DISTURB ME WHEN I AM IN HERE! YOUR UNTIMELY ENTRANCE MAY VERY WELL HAVE RUINED *WEEKS* OF WORK!

BUT-- BUT--

THERE ARE NO BUTS ABOUT IT, SON. YOU MUST --

I *TOLD* HIM TO COME GET YOU, TYRUS.

WE HAVE A *DISTRESS* CALL FROM A NEARBY SHIP.

PERHAPS YOUR TIME WOULD BE BETTER SERVED INVESTIGATING IT, INSTEAD OF YELLING AT YOUR SON, HMMM?

HRMPH!

REALLY TYRUS, YOU'RE TOO HARD ON HIM SOMETIMES.

THIS MISSION HAS BEEN DIFFICULT FOR ALL OF US, BUT *ESPECIALLY* HIM.

HE HAS NO CHILDREN HIS OWN AGE TO PLAY WITH AND --

WE'VE BEEN THROUGH ALL THIS BEFORE, *ULARA.*

WHEN WE ALL ACCEPTED THIS JOURNEY OF SPACE EXPLORATION IN THE NAME OF OUR HOMEWORLD, WE KNEW *SACRIFICES* WOULD HAVE TO BE MADE.

IT IS *DANGEROUS* OUT HERE, *ALARA,* SO IF I AM DEMANDING...

...IT IS BECAUSE I CANNOT AFFORD *NOT* TO BE.

FATHER, FATHER, ARE WE GONNA SAVE THE SHIP NOW?

WE SHALL SEE, LITTLE ONE. WE'RE COMING INTO RANGE NOW...

CONTINUED ON PAGE 24

GUARDIAN

REAL NAME: Dr. James Hudson

ABILITIES:

- **Powerful battle suit**
- **Enhanced endurance and strength**
- **Powerful force field, energy blasts, teleportation and flight.**

BACKGROUND>>>

James Hudson helped found Department H, a top-secret research and development agency for the Canadian government. Here he fell in love with and married Heather McNeil.

Shortly after, Hudson founded the team of superheroes, code-named Alpha Flight. Wolverine was to be the team's leader, however, when he quit to join the X-Men, Hudson, code-named Weapon Alpha, was ordered by his government to return him to Department H by force. He attacked Wolverine at the X-Mansion but was driven off by the combined might of the X-Men.

After Department H accepted Wolverine's resignation, Hudson and Wolverine were able to resume their friendship.

Recently, Guardian appeared to have been killed defeating his old enemy Jerome Jaxon. In truth he was teleported to an alien planet where he was bonded with his battle suit.

GUARDIAN	
STRENGTH:	8
AGILITY:	7
ENDURANCE:	5
INTELLIGENCE:	7
COMBAT SKILL:	5
POWER:	7
THREAT LEVEL:	4

SHAMAN

REAL NAME:
Dr. Michael Twoyoungmen

ABILITIES:

- **Mystical arts**
- **Levitate and fly at great speeds**
- **Cast bolts of eldritch energy and master the elements**

BACKGROUND>>>

Dr. Michael Twoyoungmen is a native Canadian and a surgeon who found that modern science was insufficient to accomplish everything he wished to do, and so he turned to the mysticism that his granfather had taught him. Becoming an accomplished adept in certain mystical arts, he was introduced to James Hudson by Hudson's wife Heather. As Shaman, Dr. Twoyoungmen became Hudson's first recruit for Alpha Flight. Since then he has remained a stalwart member and his mystical powers have proved invaluable.

SHAMAN	
STRENGTH:	4
AGILITY:	4
ENDURANCE:	5
INTELLIGENCE:	5
COMBAT SKILL:	4
POWER:	8
THREAT LEVEL:	6

PUCK

REAL NAME: Eugene Milton Judd

ABILITIES:

- **Athelete, fighter and gymnast**

BACKGROUND>>>

Eugene Judd was an adventurer, who was hired to track down the cursed Black Blade of Bagdad. However, when he found the Blade Judd accidentaly released the spirit of the evil Persian sorcerer Razer, who's soul had been imprisoned inside it. The wraith-like sorcerer began absorbing Judd's life force, at the same time causing him to shrink from his naturally tall height to 3' 4". Judd fought back and trapped Razer's spirit within him.

Years later, Judd enlisted in Gamma Flight, Department H's training super group. Judd, nicknamed 'Puck' after a hockey puck due to his small size, excelled during training and joined Alpha Flight.

Puck has remained a loyal member of the team and is close friends of James and Heather Hudson.

PUCK	
STRENGTH:	4
AGILITY:	7
ENDURANCE:	4
INTELLIGENCE:	4
COMBAT SKILL:	7
POWER:	1
THREAT LEVEL:	4

VINDICATOR

REAL NAME:
Heather McNeil Hudson

ABILITIES:
- **Powerful enrgy blasts**
- **Force Field, Teleport vast distances and flight**
- **Battle suit enhances strength and endurance**

BACKGROUND>>>
Heather McNeil fell in love and married James Hudson soon after he joined Department H. While on their honeymoon at Wood Buffalo National Park, they were attacked by Logan, who had been driven mad by the adamantium bonding process before escaping Weapon X. Heather and James nursed Logan back to health and helped him rebuild his life.

Year's later, after James Hudson was apparently killed in the process of defeating his old nemisis Jerome Jaxon, Heather was voted to become the next leader of Alpha Flight and began wearing a modified suit of James'.

OVERALL RATING 9

VINDICATOR

STRENGTH:						6				
AGILITY:							7			
ENDURANCE:					5					
INTELLIGENCE:				4						
COMBAT SKILL:			3							
POWER:							7			
THREAT LEVEL:				4						

SNOWBIRD

REAL NAME: NARYA

ABILITIES:
- **Ability to see past events**
- **Can assume the form of any creature native to the artic circle**

BACKGROUND>>>
Snowbird was born of a human father, Richard Easton, and the Eskimo goddess Nelvanna. Due to complications during the birth, Nelvanna enlisted the aid of Shaman, who was then entrusted with raising the child. Shaman named the girl Narya. The young girl grew with startling speed and at an ealry age showed signs of her shape-changing ability.

When Narya was old enough she was asked to join Alpha Flight by James Hudson where she adopted the code-name Snowbird.

SNOWBIRD

STRENGTH:				4						
AGILITY:					5					
ENDURANCE:								8		
INTELLIGENCE:			3							
COMBAT SKILL:					5					
POWER:							7			
THREAT LEVEL:							7			

OVERALL RATING 6

SASQUATCH

REAL NAME: Dr. Walter Langkowski

ABILITIES:
- **Phenomenal strength and endurance**
- **Can leap great distances**
- **Equipped with dangerous claws**

OVERALL RATING 8

BACKGROUND>>>
Walter Langkowski dedicated his life to finding a cure for Bruce Banner, better known as the Hulk. His aim was to recreate, under controlled conditions, the process that created the Hulk.

Due to the potential risk of radiation leakage, Langkowski's labratory was in a remote area of the artic circle. There he used the equipment he had designed to bombard himself with gamma radiation and was transformed into a ten-foot-tall, superhumanly powerful creature.

Afterwards, he assumed the code name Sasquatch and has become a valued member of Alpha Flight.

SASQUATCH

STRENGTH:										10
AGILITY:						6				
ENDURANCE:								8		
INTELLIGENCE:						6				
COMBAT SKILL:						6				
POWER:	1									
THREAT LEVEL:					5					

WEAPON PUZZLES X

WOLVERINE'S STRESS TEST

Alright, Bub! So ya think ya got what it takes to be the best there is? Well try your skill at these puzzles and check back with me on page 62 to see how ya did!

STRESS TEST 1 — KNOW YOUR FRIENDS AND YOUR ENEMIES >>>

In this game ya gotta now who's coverin' ya back and who's waitin to shove a knife in it! See if you can find the **10** heroes and villains listed below in the word grid.

Oh and remember, just like yer enemies who can come at yer from any direction, the names can be forwards, backwards or even diagonal!

```
Q D M B L O O D S C R E A M A
S O E C N A B V A H D N D E S
D O L R M S U E B C P A R M C
E L V E A D Q C R T L I T A K
A R E H R G D K E A R D R V O
D N I C I O E P T U V R L E L
P O T E N G A M O Q G A A R T
O L E T H C O L O S S U S I P
O S S U C R E L T A S G E C D
L A D Y D E A T H S T R I K E
```

	Heroes >>			Villains >>	
Deadpool	✓		Bloodscream	✓	
Sasquatch	✓		Omega Red	✓	
Maverick	✓		Sabretooth	✓	
Guardian	✓		Magneto	✓	
Colossus	✓		Lady Deathstrike	✓	

STRESS TEST 2 — TRACKING THE SCENT OF EVIL >>>

I've been trackin' that creep, Sabretooth's scent trough this ol' Weapon X complex but the slimeball has given me the slip! Can you help me find the correct route through the base? Just be careful, the place is crawlin' with them dirt-bag Brood, so make sure ya don't run into any of them!

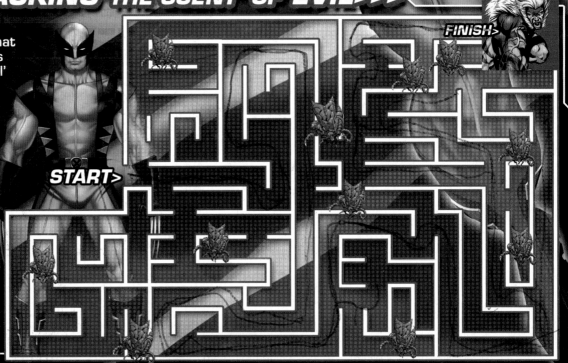

FINISH>

START>

22

THE POWER OF OBSERVATION>>>

Okay, you've tested yer wits and yer trackin', but in this business yer gotta be able to spot clues or, better yet, spot yer enemy before he spots you! So lets see how good your eyesight is. There are **10** changes in the picture below of me and my pals, the X-Men fighting those buckets of bolts, the Sentinels. See if you can find 'em all and good luck.

JUDGING BY THE **CARNAGE** LEFT IN HIS WAKE, I WAS WISE TO RECRUIT WOLVERINE.

I CAN ONLY HOPE HE SURVIVES WHAT IS YET TO COME.

IT WOULD SEEM HE MADE HIS WAY INTO THE ELEVATOR. SENSORS INDICATE A SIGNIFICANT NUMBER OF BROOD --

BEEP BEEP

WAIT. IN HIS HASTE, IT APPEARS MY COMRADE HAS LEFT ONE OF THEIR NUMBER UNACCOUNTED FOR.

THAT CANNOT BE PERMITTED. **NONE** ARE ALLOWED TO ESCAPE.

MY UNQUENCHABLE THIRST FOR VENGEANCE WILL NOT ALLOW IT.

HELLO, TYRUS.

I'VE BEEN **EXPECTING** YOU.

DO I **REMIND** YOU OF SOMEONE?

YOUR **SON**, PERHAPS?

HE WAS ABOUT MY AGE WHEN WE TOOK HIM, WAS HE NOT?

MY AGE, WHEN YOU FAILED TO **SAVE** HIM.

FAILED TO SAVE HIM, AND THE **REST** OF YOUR FAMILY.

I -- I...

YOU WERE POWERLESS TO STOP US THEN --

CONTINUED ON PAGE 35

MAGNETO

Magnetic powers

REAL NAME: UNREVEALED
PUBLIC IDENTITY: Erik Magnus Lensherr, formerly Nestor, Erik the Red, Grey King, White King and many other
HEIGHT: 6 feet 2 inches

BACKGROUND>>>
As a young man 'Eric Lensherr' befriended a young Charles Xavier. Unfortunately, the two men had radically different views on the future of their fellow mutants. Where Xavier believed in peaceful coexistence, Eric decided that the only hope for mutants was to enslave mankind. He assumed the name Magneto and has remained the X-Men's bitterest enemy. During one deadly confrontation with the X-Men, Magneto forcibly removed the adamantium from Wolverine's skeleton, triggering the X-Man's healing factor to reach its full potential and for him to evolve into a more savage, feral state.

Magneto rips the adamantium from Wolverine's body!

Magneto's powers generate powerful magnetic fields enabling him to unleash blasts of energy, fly, generate forcefields and lift vast weights

OVERALL RATING 9

MAGNETO								
STRENGTH:				4				
AGILITY:					5			
ENDURANCE:						6		
INTELLIGENCE:							7	
COMBAT SKILL:				4				
POWER:								8
THREAT LEVEL:								9

LADY DEATHSTRIKE

Extendable cybernteic claws

Superhuman strength and cyberntic senses

Adamantium skeleton

OVERALL RATING 6

NAME: YURIKO OYAMA
KNOWN ALIASES: None
HEIGHT: 5 feet 9 inches

BACKGROUND>>>
Yuriko Oyama was the daughter of the late Lord Dark Wind, a Japanese scientist who developed the process for bonding the unbreakable metal adamantium to human bone.
Believing that her father's process had been stolen and used on Wolverine's skeleton, Lady Deathstrike conceived an irrational hatred for the X-Man – determined to kill him and claim his skeleton. She was converted into a cyborg by the cyborg scientist Donald Pierce, leader of the cyborg mercenaries the Reavers and the extra-dimensional surgeon known as Spiral. Her skeleton was laced with adamantium, and she was endowed with razor-sharp, extendable claws on each hand.
Lady Deathstrike joined Pierce's Reavers and fought the X-Men on numerous occasions and every encounter she was even more determined to slay Wolverine – she has yet to achieve her goal.

LADY DEATHSTRIKE								
STRENGTH:						6		
AGILITY:					5			
ENDURANCE:						6		
INTELLIGENCE:			3					
COMBAT SKILL:								8
POWER:	1							
THREAT LEVEL:						6		

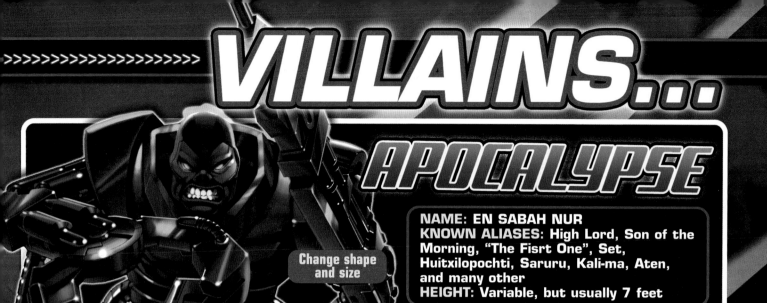

APOCALYPSE

Change shape and size

Can create weapons

Phenomenal Strength

NAME: EN SABAH NUR
KNOWN ALIASES: High Lord, Son of the Morning, "The Fisrt One", Set, Huitxilopochti, Saruru, Kali-ma, Aten, and many other
HEIGHT: Variable, but usually 7 feet

OVERALL
RATING
10

APOCALYPSE

STRENGTH:									10
AGILITY:					5				
ENDURANCE:									10
INTELLIGENCE:								9	
COMBAT SKILL:					6				
POWER:								8	
THREAT LEVEL:									10

Wolverine is revealed as Apocalypse's Horseman, Death!

BACKGROUND>>>
Apocalypse was born in ancient Egypt, around 5,000 years ago.

He has dedicated the long centuries of his life to 'culling the weak from the strong', aided by his henchmen – the Four Horseman of the Apocalypse: War, Death, Pestilence and Famine – determined that only the strongest should survive. This goal has brought him into conflict with Wolverine and the X-Men on many occasions.

In recent years, Wolverine was brainwashed by Apocalypse and became his Horseman, Death. However, Wolverine's service to Apocalypse was brief, as he ultimately regained his personality and rejoined the X-Men.

OMEGA RED

Air born 'Death Factor' drains life

Superhuman strength

Carbonadium coils

NAME: ARKADY GREGORIVICH
KNOWN ALIASES: Arkady Rossovich, Vasyliev Arkady
HEIGHT: 6 feet 11 inches

BACKGROUND>>>
Arkady Gregorivich was a serial killer in his native Russia. He was captured by the KGB, who set about transforming him into a super-soldier, code-named Omega Red. Team X, the elite covert unit that consisted of Wolverine, Sabretooth and Maverick, interrupted the procedure and stole the Carbonadium Synthesizer, a device that was used to stabilise Omega Red's mutant power and as a result the KGB placed Omega Red in suspended animation. In recent years, the criminal ninja clan the Hand mystically revived Omega Red. He allied himself with the Hand in return for the whereabouts of Wolverine and C-Synthesizer. Seeking revenge, Omega Red clashed with Wolverine and Maverick, but was defeated by Wolverine's teammates the X-Men. Since then Omega Red has fought with Wolverine on numerous occasions, even allying himself with Sabretooth and Lady Deathstrike. None of his attempts at vengeance, however, have succeeded.

OVERALL
RATING
8

OMEGA RED

STRENGTH:						6			
AGILITY:									
ENDURANCE:								8	
INTELLIGENCE:			3						
COMBAT SKILL:						6			
POWER:							7		
THREAT LEVEL:							7		

The origins of the clandestine Weapon X program date back to 1945 when the American military liberated a concentration camp and discovered the hidden laboratory of the mysterious and cruel geneticist Mister Sinister.

The insane geneticist, **Mister Sinister.**

Using Sinister's research as the basis for his own work, Professor Thornton, known simply as the Professor, formed the Weapon Plus Program at the request of the U.S. Government. Weapon Plus was dedicated to creating super-soldiers and over the next fifteen years progressed from using animals as test subjects, as in the case of Weapon II and III, to finally using mutants as the preferred test subjects.

The control room of **Weapon X** where **the Professor** and **Doctor Cornelius** monitored Wolverine's progress.

By the 1960s, the Program had advanced to Weapon X and operated under the guidance of the Central Intelligence Agency. Several mutant operatives were organised as the covert operations unit Team X, including Wolverine, Sabretooth and Maverick and a female operative called Silver Fox. All members were implanted with false memories in order to suppress their true memories and awareness of their abilities so that they could become 'sleeper' agents – agents who could integrate into society undetected and be 'awakened' when needed. In addition, Team X members also received age suppression and healing factor treatments based on Wolverine's own mutant power.

The cruel mastermind behind **Weapon X**, the Professor.

By the 1970s, Weapon X was under the direction of the Professor, assisted by Doctor Abraham Cornelius, who was wanted by the Federal Bureau of Investigations for questioning regarding so-called 'mercy killings'. The Professor chose Wolverine as his first test subject and he was kidnapped and brought to a secret facility in Canada. Here Wolverine was subjected to a brutal process that bonded the near-indestructible alloy adamantium to his skeleton and mutant claws. The Professor was surprised at the full extent of Wolverine's mutant healing factor, which enabled him to recover from the process more rapidly than anticipated. Reduced to a quasi-mindless state, Wolverine was at first pitted against wolves, a bear and even a tiger, before the ultimate test where he was sent to slaughter the inhabitants of the small town of Roanoke. However, Wolverine eventually broke free of the Professor's conditioning and ran amok in the Weapon X facility and in the course of his escape he slew most of the staff and savagely butchered a guard named Malcolm Colcord. Miraculously, Colcord survived, but he kept his horrifically scarred face as a visual reminder of his hatred for Wolverine.

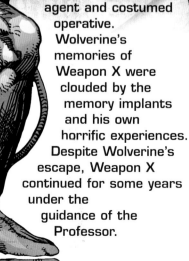

Wolverine was subsequently found by Department H's director James Hudson and his wife Heather, who nursed him back to health; he soon joined the Department as both an espionage agent and costumed operative. Wolverine's memories of Weapon X were clouded by the memory implants and his own horrific experiences. Despite Wolverine's escape, Weapon X continued for some years under the guidance of the Professor.

>>>>>>>>>>>>>>>>>>>>>>>>>>>

In recent years, Wolverine's memories of his treatment at Weapon X began to return. He sought out the Professor only to find that he had been slain by Silver Fox, now a high-ranking operative of the terrorist organisation Hydra. The Professor's associate, Cornelius died shortly afterwards at the hands of Maverick, now known as Agent Zero.

⊗ Wolverine breaks lose!

⊗ Wolverine endures excruciating pain as the indestructible alloy adamantium is bonded to his skeleton.

⊗ The beautiful but deadly **Hydra** assassin and former **Team X** operative, **Silver Fox.**

Colcord subsequently recruited several other operatives for Weapon X, all of whom he equipped with implants preventing them from turning on him or other high-ranking personnel. Colcord then opened the Neverland concentration camp where mutants who were deemed useful were utilised as support staff and those who were not were executed.

⊗ Malcom Colcord, the **Director** of the new **Weapon X.**

Weapon X's activities came to the attention of the mutant time-traveller Cable, who organised an underground movement to oppose them. However, former S.H.I.E.L.D. agent and Colcord's right hand man, Brent Jackson betrayed the Director and manipulated Cable's forces into storming the Weapon X facility, forcing Colcord to flee, only for Jackson to betray Cable and his troops in return. Jackson was soon made the new Director, but he remained unaware that one of the scientists at Neverland, Doctor Charles Windsor, was in fact a disguised Mister Sinister, ironically using this outgrowth of his past work to further his own experiments.

Soon after, Colcord returned and regained control of Weapon X. Consequently, Agent Jackson went into hiding and has not been heard of since.

Currently, Weapon X remains active as it pursues its goal of creating the perfect super-soldier.

With his death, Weapon X was apparently abandoned as a new program Weapon Plus had superseded it. Meanwhile, the head of Weapon Plus, John Sublime contacted Malcolm Colcord and persuaded him to lobby for the reopening of the U.S. Weapon X program. Colcord was successful and became the Program's new director.

Investigating the resources of the Program's earlier incarnation, Colcord discovered the means by which Wolverine had previously been mentally controlled, and directed the X-Man into stalking former Weapon X operatives, who were either recruited or slain by Colcord's forces. Among the first to rejoin was Wolverine's arch-nemesis, the savage feral mutant Sabretooth. Wolverine ultimately broke free of Colcord's control.

⊗ The treachoreous **Agent Jackson,** and former head of **Weapon X.**

ART X-TREME >>>

Hey, Bub!
Grab your pens and
learn how to draw the
ol' Canuckle head!

Copy the image above square-by-
square into the empty grid, and
then colour it in by following the
color guide!

colour guide

34

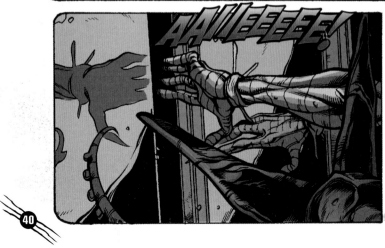

THE PAST.

BEEN... INFECTED.

FATHER!

FATHER!

MY FAMILY... MUST *HELP* THEM...

CHANGING... INTO BROOD... HYPO-SPRAY... ONLY *CHANCE!*

FSST

I DID IT! THE DEPRESSANT IN THE COMPOUND HALTED MY TRANSFORMATION.

FATHER!

I'M COMING...!

NOW, IF I AM CORRECT, THE BROOD SYSTEM CANNOT HANDLE SUCH A POWERFUL DOSE OF DEPRESSANT.

FSST

FSST

FSST

CLAW MARKS

IT IS WHAT CAUSED ME TO REVERT BACK TO MYSELF AND SHOULD CAUSE THESE BROOD TO REVERT BACK TO THEIR ORIGINAL FORMS, AS WELL.

OR IN THIS CASE, SHRIVEL UP IF A PRE-EXISTING FORM NO LONGER REMAINS.

WHATEVER THE CASE MAY BE, IT *WORKED*.

ULARA! ZET! JEXIA! WHERE ARE YOU? IT IS *SAFE* TO COME OUT NOW!

OH, NO...!

CONTINUED ON PAGE 53

47

DEADPOOL

REAL NAME: JACK
(Full Name Unreveled)
ALIASES:
Wade T. Wilson
ABILITIES:

- **Healing factor, hand-to-hand combat expert and marksman**

BACKGROUND>>>

The youth named Jack was a mercenary that frequently used plastic surgery and technology to change his identity.

As an adult, now calling himself Wade Wilson, he discovered that he had cancer and was offered hope by Weapon X; his cancer was temporarily arrested via the implantation of a healing factor derived from Wolverine. In return, Wade became a member of Weapon X.

Sometime later, Wilson's health worsened and he was sent to the Hospice, a facility where superhuman operatives were treated. In reality, Doctor Killebrew and his assistant the Attending used the Hospice's patients as experimental subjects. Wilson was subjected to many tortures, but due to his formidable strength of will, and by taunting the Attending, he survived. In revenge the Attending lobotomised one of Wilson's friends and Wilson was forced to kill him to end his suffering. However, under Killebrew's rules any patient who killed another was to be executed; the Attending tore out Wilson's heart and left him for dead, but Wilson's thirst for vengeance was so strong that it jumpstarted his healing factor, although not curing his horrifically scarred body. Wilson killed the Attending, escaped the Hospice and, assuming the name Deadpool, resumed his mercenary lifestyle – even battling Wolverine on occasion.

Over the years Deadpool has proved a fickle ally, sometimes fighting alongside Wolverine and more often against.

OVERALL RATING 7

DEADPOOL									
STRENGTH:					5				
AGILITY:						6			
ENDURANCE:					5				
INTELLIGENCE:					5				
COMBAT SKILL:									9
POWER:	1								
THREAT LEVEL:								7	

AGENT ZERO

REAL NAME:
CHRISTOPH NORD
ALIASES:
Maverick
ABILITIES:

- **Able to absorb kinetic energy and project concussive/corrosive blasts**

BACKGROUND>>>

Born in East Germany, Nord became a volunteer for the Weapon X program where he was assigned to Team X, changed his name to David North and assumed the code-name Maverick.

In recent years, when the ninja clan the Hand and former Weapon X scientist Dr. Cornelius ressurected Omega Red and captured Wolverine and his fellow X-Men, Maverick was instrumental in their rescue.

Soon after, Maverick then assisted the X-Men in capturing Sabretooth. Unfortunately, he discovered that he had contracted the deadly mutant-killing Legacy Virus and asked Wolverine to kill him in order to avoid the prolonged suffering. Wolverine refused and Maverick accepted his fate.

During the final stages of his infection, Maverick encountered the Russian mutant telepath Elena Ivanova. The virus claimed Maverick's life, but Ivanova used her powers to resurrect him as well as curing him.

Some time afterwards, during an encounter with Russian mercenaries Hammer and Sickle, Maverick lost an eye. He later resurfaced and aided Wolverine against a revived Weapon X Program. This new Program sent Sabretooth to recruit both Maverick and fellow former Team X member John Wraith. Neither accepted, and Sabretooth killed Wraith and critically injured Maverick. Brought to the Program with minutes to live, he reluctantly joined and was genetically modified to become Agent Zero.

Agent Zero, was the sent to by the Director of Weapon X to assassinate Wolverine, but he deliberately failed the mission.

OVERALL RATING 7

AGENT ZERO									
STRENGTH:				4					
AGILITY:				4					
ENDURANCE:					5				
INTELLIGENCE:					5				
COMBAT SKILL:				4					
POWER:								8	
THREAT LEVEL:						6			

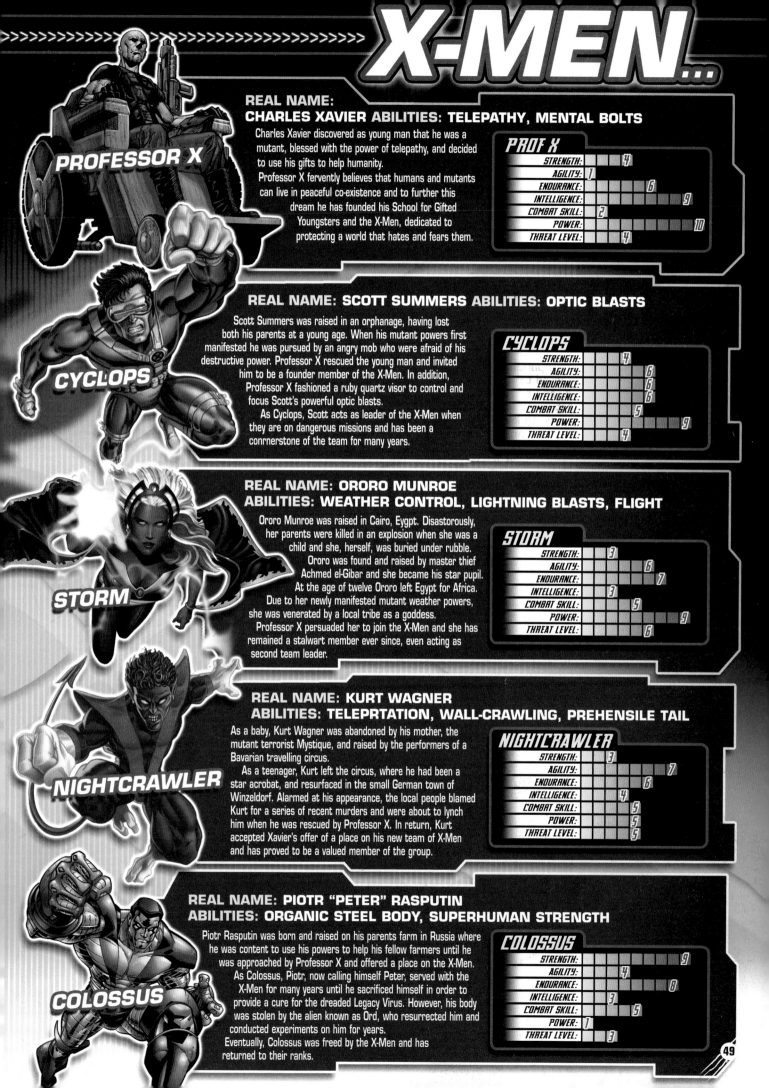

PROFESSOR X

REAL NAME:
CHARLES XAVIER ABILITIES: TELEPATHY, MENTAL BOLTS

Charles Xavier discovered as young man that he was a mutant, blessed with the power of telepathy, and decided to use his gifts to help humanity.

Professor X fervently believes that humans and mutants can live in peaceful co-existence and to further this dream he has founded his School for Gifted Youngsters and the X-Men, dedicated to protecting a world that hates and fears them.

PROF X

STRENGTH:	4
AGILITY:	1
ENDURANCE:	6
INTELLIGENCE:	9
COMBAT SKILL:	2
POWER:	10
THREAT LEVEL:	4

CYCLOPS

REAL NAME: SCOTT SUMMERS ABILITIES: OPTIC BLASTS

Scott Summers was raised in an orphanage, having lost both his parents at a young age. When his mutant powers first manifested he was pursued by an angry mob who were afraid of his destructive power. Professor X rescued the young man and invited him to be a founder member of the X-Men. In addition, Professor X fashioned a ruby quartz visor to control and focus Scott's powerful optic blasts.

As Cyclops, Scott acts as leader of the X-Men when they are on dangerous missions and has been a conrnerstone of the team for many years.

CYCLOPS

STRENGTH:	4
AGILITY:	6
ENDURANCE:	6
INTELLIGENCE:	6
COMBAT SKILL:	5
POWER:	9
THREAT LEVEL:	4

STORM

REAL NAME: ORORO MUNROE
ABILITIES: WEATHER CONTROL, LIGHTNING BLASTS, FLIGHT

Ororo Munroe was raised in Cairo, Eygpt. Disastorously, her parents were killed in an explosion when she was a child and she, herself, was buried under rubble.

Ororo was found and raised by master thief Achmed el-Gibar and she became his star pupil. At the age of twelve Ororo left Egypt for Africa. Due to her newly manifested mutant weather powers, she was venerated by a local tribe as a goddess.

Professor X persuaded her to join the X-Men and she has remained a stalwart member ever since, even acting as second team leader.

STORM

STRENGTH:	3
AGILITY:	6
ENDURANCE:	7
INTELLIGENCE:	3
COMBAT SKILL:	5
POWER:	9
THREAT LEVEL:	6

NIGHTCRAWLER

REAL NAME: KURT WAGNER
ABILITIES: TELEPRTATION, WALL-CRAWLING, PREHENSILE TAIL

As a baby, Kurt Wagner was abandoned by his mother, the mutant terrorist Mystique, and raised by the performers of a Bavarian travelling circus.

As a teenager, Kurt left the circus, where he had been a star acrobat, and resurfaced in the small German town of Winzeldorf. Alarmed at his appearance, the local people blamed Kurt for a series of recent murders and were about to lynch him when he was rescued by Professor X. In return, Kurt accepted Xavier's offer of a place on his new team of X-Men and has proved to be a valued member of the group.

NIGHTCRAWLER

STRENGTH:	3
AGILITY:	7
ENDURANCE:	6
INTELLIGENCE:	4
COMBAT SKILL:	5
POWER:	5
THREAT LEVEL:	5

COLOSSUS

REAL NAME: PIOTR "PETER" RASPUTIN
ABILITIES: ORGANIC STEEL BODY, SUPERHUMAN STRENGTH

Piotr Rasputin was born and raised on his parents farm in Russia where he was content to use his powers to help his fellow farmers until he was approached by Professor X and offered a place on the X-Men. As Colossus, Piotr, now calling himself Peter, served with the X-Men for many years until he sacrificed himself in order to provide a cure for the dreaded Legacy Virus. However, his body was stolen by the alien known as Ord, who resurrected him and conducted experiments on him for years.

Eventually, Colossus was freed by the X-Men and has returned to their ranks.

COLOSSUS

STRENGTH:	9
AGILITY:	4
ENDURANCE:	8
INTELLIGENCE:	3
COMBAT SKILL:	5
POWER:	1
THREAT LEVEL:	3

ESCAPE FROM WEAPON X

Okay, Bub! Here's yer chance to really test yer skills and help me escape from those creeps at Weapon X. All ya need is an ordinary dice and something to use as a counter. Roll the dice and move that many spaces and follow any instructions on the square. See how quickly ya can reach the X-Mansion. If you want a real challenge why not play against yer friends.

START

1

2

3

4

26 Attacked by Sabretooth! Go back to space 19

25

29

28

27

35 Attacked by Omega Red! Go back to space 28.

33

34

30 Teleported by Nightcrawler! Take 2 turns.

32

36

31

37 Attacked by Sentinels! Miss 2 turns

38

Grab your pens and add some colour so that WOLVERINE can defeat The BROOD in style!

IT'S *OVER*. HE AIN'T GETTIN' UP FROM *THAT*.

DIDN'T HAVE T' END THIS WAY, KRILL.

I AM AFRAID IT *DID*.

I JUST GOT ONE QUESTION, BUB. *WHY?*

I MUST CONFESS, MY FRIEND, I HAVE NOT BEEN COMPLETELY *HONEST* WITH YOU.

I KINDA FIGURED *THAT* OUT BY NOW.

"TRUTH BE TOLD, WHEN I ENTERED THE ESCAPE HATCH AFTER THE BROOD ATTACK ON MY FAMILY, I MADE A STARTLING DISCOVERY.

"MY FAMILY HAD BEEN CHANGED, TURNED INTO THE VERY MONSTROSITIES WE *BATTLED* THAT DAY.

"I WAS DEVASTATED. BETTER THEY HAD *DIED* THAN TO GO ON LIVING SUCH AN UNHOLY EXISTENCE.

"I *RAN*, WANTING TO ESCAPE THE LIVING NIGHTMARE THAT WAS THERE BEFORE MY EYES.

"THEY CLOSED THE HATCH BEHIND ME AND JETTISONED THE POD.

"I WOULD NEVER SEE THEM AS I KNEW THEM AGAIN."

SO YOU SEE, WHAT I AM TRYING TO TELL YOU...

THESE BROOD DIDN'T *KILL* MY FAMILY --

-- THEY *WERE* MY FAMILY.

I MADE A VOW THAT DAY THAT I WOULD NOT REST UNTIL MY FAMILY WERE PUT OUT OF THEIR MISERY.

THE PROBLEM WAS, I TOO WAS INFECTED FIGHTING THE BROOD.

I TOO *SHARE* THEIR FINAL FATE.

IT IS WHY I BROUGHT YOU HERE, WHY I ATTACKED YOU, TO *FINISH* WHAT I COULD NOT.

I OWE YOU A DEBT, WOLVERINE, ONE I CAN NEVER REPAY.

Alright, Bub! Check the answers below and lets see how ya did

STRESS TEST 1

STRESS TEST 2

FINISH>

STRESS TEST 3

Claw Mark observation test.

Okay! Didja spot all my claw marks? If ya missed any have another look before I tell ya where they are.

CLAW MARKS

They were on pages 11, 18, 23, 25, 35, 40, 47, 55, and 58.

62